WONDER WOMAN™

IN

CHEETAH ON THE PROWL

Story by Andrew Helfer
Illustrated by Ross Andru, Dick Giordano and Carl Gafford

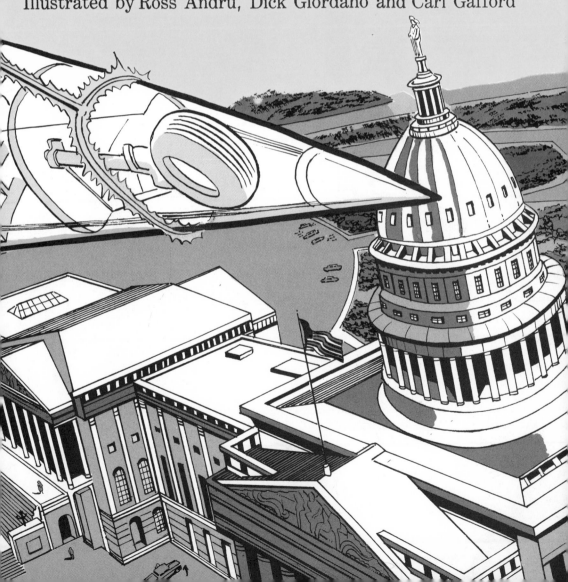

Far from civilization, hidden deep within the Bermuda
Triangle, there is an island unlike any other. It is called
Paradise Island, and, true to its name, it is a paradise.
Only women live on this island—a race of females who are
as beautiful as they are powerful. They are called Amazons,
and the Gods who watch over them have taught them how
to live peacefully and happily with one another.

At the top of Paradise Island's highest peak stands a
majestic temple. It was there that Hippolyta, Queen of the
Amazons, called to the Gods.

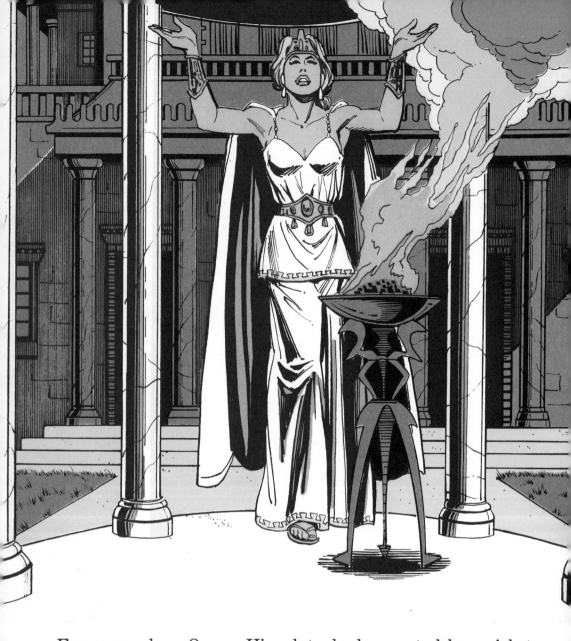

For many days Queen Hippolyta had repeated her wish to Aphrodite, the beautiful Goddess of Love, but she never received a reply. Still, the noble Queen refused to give up hope, and each day returned to her mountaintop temple. There, she pleaded to the sky:

"Please, O Goddess, appear before me. There is something I need to ask of you. Please—your willing and faithful servant calls you!"

Suddenly, the cloud of smoke rising from the temple altar seemed to grow bigger, filling the room with billows of grey mist. Then a shadowy figure appeared in the center of the smoke. It was Aphrodite, The Goddess of Love! She had finally come!

"Why do you call me now, Hippolyta, Queen of my people?" the Goddess asked.

"I need to learn the secret of modeling life from the enchanted clay," the Queen replied. "There are no children here on Paradise Island, and the Amazons will need a Princess to rule this land when I am away."

The misty figure hung silently in the air for a moment, thinking. Then the Goddess spoke again:

"Take the enchanted clay and model the figure of the child you want. When it is complete, I shall return to fulfill your wish."

Then, in a swirl of smoke, the Goddess vanished.

7

As the days passed, Hippolyta worked long and hard on the clay statue of the child. Often she sculpted late into the night, making sure each detail on the figure was just right.

"She will be my daughter," Hippolyta mused, "and someday she will be Queen of the Amazons. She must be perfect."

Her work finished, Hippolyta returned to the temple altar, placing the clay figure of the child in its center. Again, she prayed to the Goddess of Love:

"Aphrodite, I have done as you have commanded. The child is complete—and she is very beautiful. Now, O Goddess, please touch her with your gift of life!"

The figure on the pedestal began to change before the Queen's astonished eyes. The clay seemed to soften, to ripple with life, as its color changed from a lifeless grey to a warm pink! Then, it began to move!

"Goddess be praised!" Hippolyta whispered in a thankful voice, as the happy child jumped from the pedestal into her mother's arms. Overjoyed, Hippolyta spoke to the child:

"You are my daughter, and one day you will be Queen of Paradise Island. I shall name you Diana, after the Goddess of the Hunt. Your strength and beauty will be greater than that of any other Amazon!"

Although she was only minutes old, the little Amazon seemed to understand the Queen's every word.

It took only a short time for the women of Paradise Island to know and love the newest addition to their homeland...

HIPPOLYTA MUST BE VERY PROUD OF THE YOUNG PRINCESS THAT APHRODITE HAS GIVEN HER!

YES -- THE CHILD GROWS STRONGER AND MORE BEAUTIFUL WITH EACH PASSING DAY!

Indeed, the young Diana was a *truly* Amazing Amazon. Within weeks of her arrival she was already strong enough to uproot the mightiest tree...

....and the loyal and happy subjects of Paradise Island would often see her frolicking through the forest with the island's wildlife. The child could outrace the swiftest deer, without even losing her breath.

It was clear to all who witnessed each of the Princess' astounding feats that she was destined to be the greatest Amazon they had ever known.

Years passed, and Princess Diana's intelligence, agility and beauty increased by leaps and bounds. Before the women of Paradise Island knew it...

...their precious little Princess had matured into a confident, independent woman. Although she did not yet wear the world-famous Wonder Woman costume, to the Amazons she was a wonder just the same!

Then one day something happened that would forever change the life of Princess Diana. An airplane mysteriously crashed into the churning waters just off the beautiful island's coast. Diana and a friend were standing on one of Paradise Island's many cliffs when the aircraft smacked into the sea with a thunderous force. Diana was startled, but what she saw next sent her into action!

Floating on a piece of the plane's wreckage was the still body of its pilot. Head covered with a protective helmet, the fallen flyer did not move as the waves slapped angrily against the slowly sinking debris.

"She must be badly hurt!" Diana shouted to her friend, her voice nervous, yet determined. "We must help her!"

Then without a pause, the courageous Amazon Princess leapt from the cliff towards the violent waters below!

I'VE GOT TO SAVE HER BEFORE SHE DROWNS!

Swimming against the swirling current, it took almost all of Diana's strength to reach the unconscious form.

With the pilot held
tightly in one arm, Diana
slowly swam toward
shore...

SHE'S BARELY ALIVE! I
HOPE I CAN GET BACK IN
TIME TO SAVE HER!

Once on the beach, Diana prepared to give the pilot
artificial respiration. But when she removed the helmet, both
Amazons were stunned!

W-WHY--
SHE'S NOT
A WOMAN
AT ALL!
WHAT KIND
OF HUMAN
IS THAT?

I-I THINK IT'S A MAN!
MOTHER TOLD ME ABOUT THEM!
BUT I'VE NEVER SEEN ONE
MYSELF! H-HE'S QUITE HANDSOME!
BUT MAN OR WOMAN WE'VE GOT
TO GET HELP! HE'S
BARELY ALIVE!

Without a moment's hesitation, Diana carried the pilot to the island's hospital. There, using advanced medical treatments and machinery, a team of Amazon doctors worked frantically to save the man's faltering life.

"The tags around his neck say his name is Steve Trevor," Diana said softly to the busy physicians. "Please tell me—will he live?"

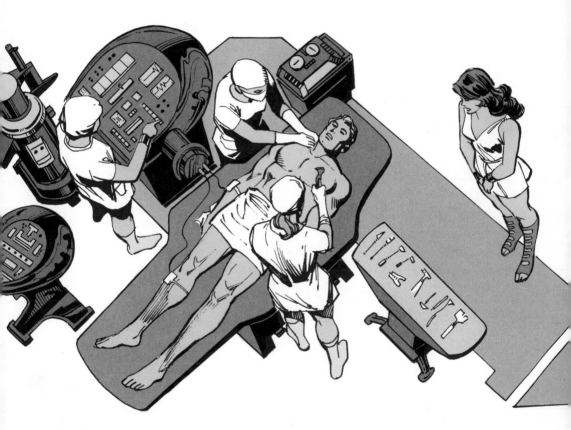

"We're doing all we can to save him," one of the doctors replied. "But he's swallowed a lot of water. We've done our best; the rest is up to him." The doctor looked up at Diana and saw the sorrow in her eyes. "Princess, there's nothing you can do here," she said kindly.

But Diana would not leave. "I'd like to stay by his side, if you don't mind," she said as she solemnly gazed at the still body of Colonel Steve Trevor.

Queen Hippolyta watched the scene unfolding in the hospital from the monitor in her throne room. She could not fail to notice the twinkle of love in Princess Diana's eyes. Deeply troubled, Hippolyta called to the Goddess of Love, asking for her guidance:

"The unspeakable has happened. For the first time in untold centuries, a man has come to Paradise Island. Already our lives have been changed—my daughter has begun to feel *love* for the one known as Steve Trevor! Aphrodite, has this man come to destroy our peaceful lives here?"

Suddenly, a cool, misty breeze swept through the room, and the Goddess Aphrodite appeared:

"Be silent, my Queen, and I shall put your fears to rest. *I* have sent the man called Steve Trevor to your island of Amazons, and with good reason. The world outside is torn with war and hate, and the future of the very planet is at stake. Steve Trevor *will* live to go back to his homeland, but he must be accompanied by your strongest and wisest subject."

SELECT YOUR CHAMPION, HIPPOLYTA, FOR SHE MUST JOIN MANKIND TO COMBAT ALL THE EVILS THAT THREATEN TO DESTROY THE PEACE OF THE ENTIRE EARTH!

The next day, Queen Hippolyta announced the contest to decide which Amazon would take Steve Trevor back to his homeland, a place called the United States. After the proclamation had been made, Hippolyta called Diana to her side.

"Diana," she said sternly, "I forbid you to enter the tournament. It is your destiny to rule Paradise Island. If you were to win and leave with Colonel Trevor, your fellow Amazons might someday be left without a leader. I'm sorry, but my decision is final."

But outside the throne room Diana came up with an idea:

"I hate to go against my mother's wishes, but I can't bear to let Steve Trevor return to his society with anyone but me. I'll disguise myself so mother won't recognize me! Then I'll be able to enter the contest!"

The next morning the games began. Trumpets blared as the group of competing Amazons entered the stadium. Each Amazon was proud to be a part of the contest, but as they walked by Hippolyta's throne, the Queen noticed that one contestant wore a mask to hide her identity.

No one knew that Princess Diana had entered the contest. And only a few noticed the mystery contestant among the other hopefuls. But soon, *every* Amazon would wonder who she was.

As soon as the contests began, the audience knew what the final outcome would be. The mystery contestant won every possible test, from wrestling and running, to jousting and the boomerang toss. No other Amazon could come close to beating her in even a single event. This masked marvel was truly the Amazon champion.

At the close of the contest, Hippolyta awarded the Crown of Victory to the masked champion.

"Congratulations," the Queen said. "You have proven yourself to be the strongest and most agile of all the Amazons. Now is the time to show us who you really are."

With a flick of her wrist, Princess
Diana removed her mask, revealing
herself to the Queen.

"Daughter…it—it's you!!"

"Yes mother," Diana answered,
feeling guilty, yet determined to do
what she thought was right. "I'm
sorry, but this is something I have
to do. I love Steve Trevor, and I
must return to the United States
with him. I know my happy life here
with the Amazons is over, but it is
now my duty to save the world from
destruction."

Hippolyta thought for a moment, considering the courageous
woman who stood before her. Forcing back her sadness, the
Queen smiled weakly and spoke:

"I am proud of you Diana—you are truly our bravest
Amazon. I made this costume for the winner to use when she
journeyed to the United States—you have won the right to
wear it with pride. There are other things I must give you,
but first," she said, turning to the crowd, "let us celebrate!"

With that, the Amazons lifted Diana onto their shoulders and paraded her proudly around the stadium. The spectators cheered wildly:

"Hooray for Princess Diana!"

"She is our champion!"

"She is our Wonder Woman!"

When the festivities were over, Diana received the gifts she would need in her battle against evil. First, Hippolyta gave her a magic lariat that would make any person roped within it follow the Princess' every command. Then the Queen pointed to the sky, where a beautiful transparent plane hovered silently over the assembled Amazons.

"You will use this Robot Plane to take Steve Trevor home. He is already inside. The plane cannot be seen by mortal eyes, and it makes no sound. You have but to give it an order, and it will obey."

A tear began to form in Hippolyta's eye as Diana prepared to leave. She was going to miss her daughter. Her voice choked with emotion, the Queen spoke for a final time:

FROM THIS DAY ON, YOU WILL BE KNOWN AS... *WONDER WOMAN!* NOW GO, MY DAUGHTER-- YOU HAVE MUCH WORK TO DO!

In moments, the Robot Plane was soaring high in the air. Wonder Woman looked back a final time to see a cheering crowd of Amazons wave goodbye.

"Perhaps this is the wrong thing I do," she thought to herself. "Perhaps I *do* belong on Paradise Island."

But one look at Steve Trevor lying silently at her side, convinced her that she was doing the right thing.

Soon the Robot Plane was hovering above an Army hospital in a city called Washington D.C. With Steve Trevor in her arms, the Amazon Princess jumped from the plane. Floating down on the air currents, she landed softly on the hospital lawn.

The hospital staff didn't know what to make of this flying woman, but when she said "This man needs your help," they rushed to assist her.

With Colonel Trevor in good hands, Wonder Woman was free to begin her mission. But she still wanted to be near the man she loved. After some thought she decided:

I'LL BECOME AN ARMY NURSE! THAT WAY I CAN SEE STEVE TREVOR EVERY DAY, AND STILL BE FREE TO COMBAT EVIL!

Now, in the identity of Lieutenant Diana Prince, Wonder Woman was able to watch Steve's condition improve, and, as his nurse, could check on him daily. Soon, Trevor was smiling and talking to Diana— mostly about the television reports he had seen, and his own faint memories of the super heroine who had brought him to the hospital. "Isn't Wonder Woman wonderful?" he would say to Diana, never knowing that he was talking to the Amazing Amazon in person!

After he recovered, Steve prepared to leave the hospital.

"Well...uh...I guess this is it, Diana."

Just then, Steve had an idea. "Say—how would you like to be my assistant? I could use someone like you. I mean, you're no Wonder Woman, but what mortal woman is?"

Diana simply smiled, and in a quiet voice said "I'll take it."

Within months, Diana had been promoted to Captain. She was proud of herself. Now she was a success in both the world of the Amazons, and in the world of Man!

Steve escorted her to her new office.

"Well, Captain—here it is," he proclaimed. "But don't get too comfortable—we're off to Montana on an intelligence mission! Be ready to fly in fifteen minutes!"

Before Diana even knew what was happening, she and Steve were whisked off on a jet bound for a secret destination in the wilds of Montana. As they prepared to land, Diana gasped in awe at the spectacular sight that was spread out before her eyes.

The white concrete buildings of Marsden Air Force Base reflected the early morning sun, sending shafts of light back into the crisp blue sky. The walls of a newly built dam, restraining tons of water, loomed over the military installation.

Only a few top officers were aware of the base's existence, and even *they* were unsure of what went on here. The whole thing was a mystery, and Diana was curious.

As Diana and Steve got off the plane, a man in a General's uniform rushed up to greet them. Diana could see that the General was very upset.

"That's General Peters," Steve whispered to Diana. "But I've never seen him look so disorganized before. Something big must be up—something that the General couldn't handle himself."

Sure enough, as the General escorted Steve and Diana through the base, he told them of the series of disasters that had perplexed everyone.

"Someone's been destroying our new test planes," the General said nervously. "We call them Dynasonics, and they are designed to be the fastest planes ever built—but they're being blown up before we can test them! We've tried to stop the saboteurs, but nothing seems to work!

"I can't trust anyone—not even the soldiers guarding the Dynasonic! I'm at the end of my rope! I need you to capture the saboteurs. I want you to *personally* guard the Dynasonic. You'll have men guarding the runway outside, but I don't want anyone except you two in the hangar with that plane!"

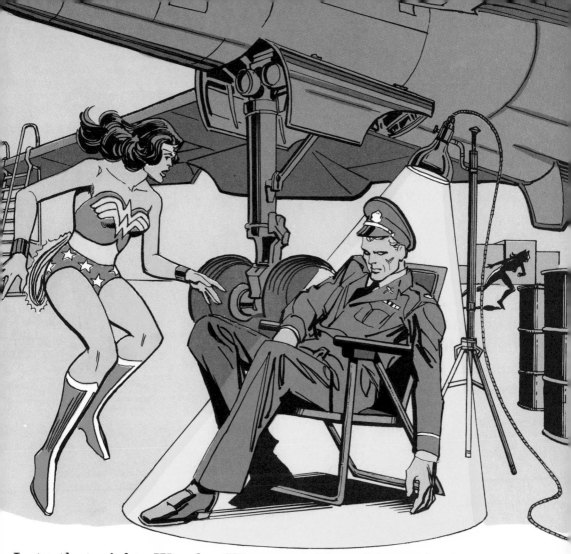

Late that night, Wonder Woman paid a visit to the hangar where the Dynasonic was kept. She knew Steve was supposed to be guarding the huge aircraft, but when she arrived, Steve appeared to be—sleeping!

Wonder Woman was worried. Steve was a top Intelligence officer; he would never fall asleep while on duty!

"This must be the work of the saboteurs!" Wonder Woman thought. "But the Dynasonic is still safe and sound!"

Puzzled as she was, the Amazon Princess did not have time to think about this strange new development. She had to make sure Steve was safe. She was so concerned that she did not notice a mysterious figure slinking out of the airplane hangar.

STEVE?--STEVE? ARE YOU ALL RIGHT? WHAT HAPPENED HERE?

With the skill of a trained nurse, Wonder Woman brought the Colonel back to consciousness. Steve's eyelids began to flutter, and as he awoke, he groaned in pain. Wonder Woman was relieved that Steve was not seriously injured, despite the large bruise on the back of his head.

OOOOOHH--MY HEAD HURTS--SOMEONE MUST HAVE HIT ME--KNOCKED ME OUT-- *THE DYNASONIC!* IS IT--?

IT'S STILL HERE, STEVE. I MUST HAVE FRIGHTENED THE SABOTEURS AWAY WHEN I WALKED IN!

Just then the cool night air was pierced by a series of high-pitched screams.

"That noise! It sounds like someone's in trouble!"

"You'd better investigate, Wonder Woman. I'll be able to guard the Dynasonic now!"

As Wonder Woman streaked out of the hangar, she noticed that the soldiers General Peters had assigned to guard the runway were nowhere to be seen.

"I hope Steve can watch the Dynasonic by himself, because I can't ignore the screams coming from those barracks over there—even if it means leaving the Dynasonic practically unguarded!"

In seconds, The Amazon Princess reached the building from which the noises were coming and burst through the door.

Inside, she was confronted by a shocking sight. The group of soldiers assigned to guard the runway were being held hostage—by a pack of ferocious mountain lions! The savage cats clawed and growled at the helpless soldiers who could do nothing more than wave sticks and chairs at the felines, and scream for help.

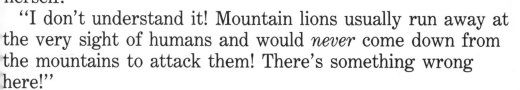

I DON'T LIKE LETTING THESE MEN THINK I'M RUNNING OUT ON THEM, BUT I'VE GOT NO CHOICE!

Without apparent reason, Wonder Woman slammed the barrack door shut, leaving the frightened men trapped inside! As she summoned her Amazon strength for a graceful leap to the roof of the building, she thought to herself:

"I don't understand it! Mountain lions usually run away at the very sight of humans and would *never* come down from the mountains to attack them! There's something wrong here!"

Once on the roof, Wonder Woman peered through the skylight. In the room below, the cats were climbing onto the table where the defenseless soldiers stood huddled in fear. There was no time to lose! In a single motion, Wonder Woman shattered the rooftop window.

Standing above the panicked soldiers, Wonder Woman twirled her magic lasso through the smashed skylight in a wide loop. As if with a life of its own, the golden-linked lariat descended, pulling itself tight around the frightened men. Then, with a single tug, Wonder Woman pulled the entire group of men up and onto the barrack roof.

"Thanks, Wonder Woman!" one of the soldiers exclaimed. "We were guarding the runway when we saw someone sneaking into this barrack, but when we got here it was empty. We were about to return to our posts when the cats greeted us at the door!"

"This has to be the work of the saboteur," Wonder Woman replied. "I'd better get back to Steve and the Dynasonic!"

Just then, a sonic boom broke through the stillness of the night air. "Look!" a soldier shouted. "It's the Dynasonic! Its been stolen!"

"SUFFERING SAPPHO!" Wonder Woman exclaimed as the top secret plane flew off into the distance. Suddenly, the truth was all too obvious—the mountain lions had been a carefully planned diversion to get both her and the soldiers away from the hangar so the saboteur could once again attempt to steal the Dynasonic!

Immediately, the Mighty Amazon summoned her Robot Plane. Seconds later she climbed onto its hanging ladder, shouting back to the safe but stranded soldiers:

"Sorry, fellows, you'll have to get off the roof by yourselves—I've got a plane to catch!"

Once inside the Invisible Plane, the Amazon Princess made radio contact with the hijacked aircraft.

"Wonder Woman to Dynasonic—come in!"

A crackling noise came over the Invisible Plane's speakers. Then a voice spoke. It was a woman's voice, and it cackled with evil glee.

"Hello, Wonder Woman," the voice hissed. "This is The Cheetah speaking. I've got the Dynasonic, and I'm afraid that you're a little too slow to stop me!"

Angrily, Wonder Woman replied to The Cheetah's boast:

"Sorry, Cheetah, I don't give up that easily. Besides, *my* plane was built by a highly advanced technology, and even now I'm gaining on you!"

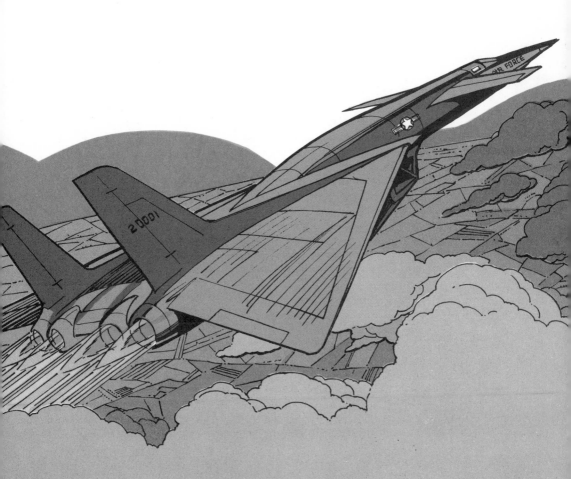

But The Cheetah was not impressed.

"Well then," she smirked, "come on over. I only hope you don't get more than you bargained for. You see, Wonder Woman, when it comes to destroying Dynasonics, I'm batting a thousand!"

Slowly but surely, the Robot Plane advanced on the Dynasonic. With a final burst of speed, the amazing aircraft swooped down, landing firmly on the stolen plane's roof.

As the wind howled mercilessly around her, Wonder Woman climbed out of the Robot Plane's cockpit. She had never ordered the Robot Plane to go *this* fast before, but the plane had done its job. Now, it was time for Wonder Woman to do *her* job. Steeling herself, she stepped out onto the Dynasonic's roof.

The Amazing Amazon was determined to get to the Dynasonic's cockpit to confront the villainous saboteur. The wind was so fierce that it took all her strength to do it.

Reaching the front of the Dynasonic, Wonder Woman shouted down to her foe: "This game of yours is just about over, Cheetah!"

But The Cheetah had an ace up her sleeve.

"I don't think so, Wonder Woman. You see, I'm going to be leaving soon. But I'd like you to meet a new 'friend' of mine. Perhaps *he* can entertain you!"

Wonder Woman heard a loud click.

Instantly, the hatch of the plane blew open, propelling the ejection-seated Cheetah into the air. Wonder Woman was about to call her Robot Plane to pursue the villainess, when she heard a cry for help coming from inside the plane:

"Wonder Woman! Help me!" The Amazon Princess recognized the voice—it was Steve Trevor!

As Wonder Woman tugged him out of the cockpit, Steve Trevor explained what had happened:

"The Cheetah was the one who knocked me out. After you left to save those men, she returned and kidnapped me to pilot the Dynasonic! She's planted a bomb on it somewhere, and it's set to go off any second now! There's no time to defuse it, so let's get out of here—fast!"

HANG ON, STEVE-- WE'LL BE OUT OF HERE IN NO TIME!

I HOPE SO -- 'CAUSE THAT'S ALL THE TIME WE HAVE!

No sooner had Steve scrambled aboard the Robot Plane than the Dynasonic exploded into a thousand metal fragments. The noise was deafening, but when it died down, the sky was completely silent.

"We've failed—the Dynasonic's been destroyed," Steve groaned.

"The Dynasonic *is* gone," Wonder Woman shouted up at the distaught Colonel, "but perhaps I can capture The Cheetah before she does any more damage."

From her perch on the Robot Plane's rope ladder Wonder Woman peered downward, her eyes searching across the scenic landscape beneath her. Before long, she spotted a slowly descending parachute in the distance.

"That has to be The Cheetah," Wonder Woman thought. "If I hurry, I might catch her before she escapes into the woods!"

Commanding the Robot Plane to take Steve back to the base, Wonder Woman leapt off the rope ladder. From his seat, Steve watched with admiration as the beautiful Amazon skillfully glided on the air currents down towards the ground.

"Good luck, Wonder Woman," Steve murmured as the Robot Plane steered itself back to the base.

Drifting downward, Wonder Woman saw no sign of The Cheetah. The villainess had vanished! But then, the Amazing Amazon saw something that seemed out of place in the wild countryside.

There, in a small clearing, lay The Cheetah's abandoned parachute. Big and white in the moonlight, it stood out like a target for the Amazon Princess to land on. And if the parachute was here, then The Cheetah could not be far away.

As the Amazing Amazon inspected the tattered remains of the parachute, she heard someone—or something—approaching through the woods. Cautiously, she looked up, and found herself eye-to-eye with four ferocious mountain lions!

"MERCIFUL MINERVA! This has got to be The Cheetah's work!" Wonder Woman thought as the beasts warily circled her, getting ready to attack. "These poor animals were lured here by The Cheetah to help in her evil scheme! I won't hurt them, but I *can* do—this!"

At super-speed, Wonder Woman whipped out her magic lasso, swinging it high over the pack of confused cats. The golden rope seemed alive as it shimmered in the moonlight, glowing with Amazon magic. Then, in a blur of motion, the Amazon Princess ensnared each of the ferocious felines, ordering them to go to sleep. A few moments later, all four were dreaming peacefully.

But this diversion had bought The Cheetah the time she needed to cover her tracks. Wonder Woman searched for the villainess, but could find her nowhere.

"...So you see, General, although we have not yet captured The Cheetah, we now know just who our saboteur is, and can work to prevent her from getting the last Dynasonic."

Wonder Woman sounded confident as she spoke, but the General was still angry.

"The fact remains," the General barked, his face pale and tired, "that you failed in your mission, Trevor, and now we have only one Dynasonic left to test! I gave Captain Prince permission to search the countryside for The Cheetah's hideout this morning, so you'll have to keep things under control here. I want no bungling this time, Colonel!"

As the General continued to shout at Steve, Wonder Woman looked around the enormous assembly plant. All around her, welders, machinists, carpenters, mechanics, and other craftsmen were doing their jobs at a frantic pace, each adding their own sound to the noisy symphony that filled the room.

"I ordered the men to speed up the production of the new Dynasonic," General Peters said, "so our final test plane should be ready by tomor...."

His words trailed off as a mysterious voice boomed over the PA system. "ATTENTION," the voice said. "I DEMAND your attention!"

All the workers stopped what they were doing. They looked stunned.

"I am called The Cheetah," the voice said without a trace of emotion, "and I have an important announcement to make!"

"Trevor! Do something!" General Peters growled.

No one moved.

No one, that is, except Wonder Woman, who bolted towards the factory doors. "She's broadcasting from somewhere on the base!" the Amazon shouted, "and I've got to capture her before she makes her next move!"

Outside, from a guard tower next to the huge dam overlooking the compound, The Cheetah began her message to the people of Marsden Air Force Base:

"For many years, man has tried to destroy his environment. Air, water, and noise pollution get worse every day. I, The Cheetah, have had enough of this. The Dynasonic is the fastest and loudest plane ever built. Its aggravating vibrations, and the sonic boom it makes, frighten my animal friends. So I destroyed your dangerous planes.

"But there is an even greater ecological menace here, and it is right in front of your pitiful eyes! It is the dam overlooking your base. It has endangered many forms of wildlife. It has forced the animals to go upstream, where food is not as plentiful. And it has blocked the river waters that once fed so many beautiful trees.

"I intend to avenge the injustices you have brought upon nature. In ten seconds, your precious dam will explode."

Suddenly, a huge explosion rocked the base. Great chunks of the concrete dam shot outward, each slab a dangerous missile large enough to destroy a part of the defenseless compound. But this was only a minor problem compared to what would happen next.

As the base personnel stared in wide-eyed horror, a torrent of angry white water began rushing through the enormous hole that the explosion had made in the dam, threatening the lives of everyone on the base!

Gliding high above the dam, Wonder Woman searched for a solution. She noticed the cracks in the remaining dam wall, and knew that at any moment the entire dam might collapse, instantly submerging the whole compound! She watched in horror as the churning water rushed up to the jagged hole in the dam, struggling to smash apart the remains of the once-mighty walls. The peaceful lake had been transformed into a raging river, almost alive in its determination to break through the concrete walls and begin a rampage of watery destruction! But then, Wonder Woman found the solution!

Faster then the eye could follow, Wonder Woman looped her magic lariat around the summit of a barren mountain looming over the dam. Then she pulled, using every ounce of her fabled strength.

At first, nothing seemed to be happening, but soon the mountaintop began to groan and quake as the lariat ripped it free from its very base!

Swinging the craggy peak high into the sky, Wonder Woman spun around, snapping the lariat like a whip. The mountaintop flew towards the dam...

...where it crashed right into the gaping hole, plugging up the waterfall that threatened to destroy the compound! Behind the dam wall the waters swirled about in confusion, and on the other side only a few drops could be seen trickling through.

"A perfect fit!" Wonder Woman declared proudly. High above the compound, she could hear the entire base breathe a sigh of relief. With the threat ended, it was time for the Amazon Princess to turn her sights to the *cause* of the near-disaster!

As Wonder Woman approached the guard tower, she spotted the Cheetah trying to make her getaway.

The Cheetah did not pause to look back as the Amazing Amazon gracefully landed on the tower ledge. She knew she was beaten. Her plan to destroy the base had failed. And as she felt the links of the magic golden lasso pull tight against her arms, all hope of escape was gone.

"Wait a second, Cheetah! You're not going anywhere, except to a nice 'cage' in a federal jail!"

As Wonder Woman and her captured foe descended to the foot of the dam, they were greeted by Steve Trevor, a *very* relieved General Peters, and a platoon of cheering soldiers.

"Three cheers for Wonder Woman," they cried. "HIP HIP HOORAY!"

Later, Wonder Woman, the General, and Steve Trevor decided what should be done with The Cheetah.

"Of course," the General said, "she must stand trial. But some of the things she said made sense. Her ideas might not be wrong, but using force never convinced *me* to change *my* opinions!"

Wonder Woman then spoke to The Cheetah:

"It's O.K. to fight for what you believe in, but you have to make sure you don't hurt others when you do it. If you do, no one will listen to your ideas, no matter how good they might be!"

Soon, Wonder Woman decided it was time to leave.

"Take care of yourself," Steve Trevor shouted as the Amazing Amazon boarded her plane. "We'll see you soon—I hope!"

Wonder Woman smiled to herself. Steve *would* be seeing her very soon indeed. But it would be as Diana Prince, Air Force Captain, rather than as Princess Diana—The Wonder Woman!